Read on a cold winter night,

Love, Great. G'ma Marilyn & Jay

THE ADVENTURES OF PINOCCHIO

The Classic Tale

THE ADVENTURES OF

PINOCCHIO

by Carlo Collodi

Illustrated by Greg Hildebrandt

COURAGE
BOOKS
AN IMPRINT OF RUNNING PRESS
PHILADELPHIA · LONDON

9   8   7   6   5   4   3   2   1
Digit on the right indicates the number of this printing

Library of Congress Control Number: 2003103748

ISBN 0-7624-1713-7

Cover illustration by Greg Hildebrandt
Cover and Interior Design by Frances J. Soo Ping Chow
Typography: Bembo and Type Embellishments
Text adapted and abridged by Elizabeth Haserick

This book may be ordered by mail from the publisher.
But try your bookstore first!

Published by Courage Books, an imprint of
Running Press Book Publishers
125 South Twenty-second Street
Philadelphia, Pennsylvania 19103-4399

Visit us on the web!
www.runningpress.com

PINOCCHIO

There once was a piece of wood, lying in the carpenter shop of Master Antonio. Master Antonio decided to make a table leg out of the wood, but to his surprise, when he struck it, the wood cried out.

Just then his friend Geppetto, a little old man with a yellow wig, came in. Whenever anyone wanted to make Geppetto angry they would just comment on his yellow wig, calling him *Polendina*, which means "yellow corn pudding".

Geppetto told Master Antonio:

"I want to make a beautiful wooden marionette. With it I intend to go around the world, to earn my living. What do you think?"

"Bravo, Polendina!" cried a tiny voice which came from no one knew where.

On hearing himself called Polendina, Master Geppetto turned red and, facing the carpenter, said to him angrily: "Why do you insult me?"

"Who is insulting you?"

"You called me Polendina."

"I did not."

"Yes."

"No."

"Yes."

"No."

And growing angrier each moment, they began to fight.

When the fight was over, Master Antonio and Geppetto agreed to be friends.

"Well then, Master Geppetto," said the carpenter, "what is it you want?"

"I want a piece of wood to make a marionette. Will you give it to me?" asked Geppetto.

Master Antonio, very glad indeed, gave Geppetto the piece of wood which had cried out. Geppetto thanked Master Antonio, and limped away toward home.

Geppetto lived in a one-room house that was neat and comfortable. The furniture was very simple: an old chair, a rickety bed, and a tumble-down table. A fireplace full of burning logs was painted on the wall opposite the door. Over the fire was painted a pot full of something, which kept boiling happily away and sending up clouds of what looked like real steam.

As soon as he reached home, Geppetto took his tools and began to cut and shape the wood into a marionette.

"What shall I call him?" he said to himself. "I think I'll call him Pinocchio. That is a lucky name."

After choosing the name for his marionette, Geppetto set to work on the hair, forehead, and eyes. Fancy his surprise when he noticed that these eyes moved and then stared at him. Geppetto, seeing this, said:

"Ugly wooden eyes, why do you stare so?"

There was no answer.

After the eyes, Geppetto made the nose, which began to stretch as soon as it was finished. It stretched until it became so long it seemed endless. Poor Geppetto kept cutting it, but the more he cut, the longer the nose grew. In despair he let it alone.

Next he made the mouth. No sooner was it finished than it began to laugh and poke fun at him.

"Stop laughing!" Geppetto yelled angrily.

The mouth stopped laughing, but it stuck out a long tongue.

Not wishing to start an argument, Geppetto made believe he saw nothing and went on with his work. After the mouth, he made the chin, then the neck, the shoulders, the stomach, the arms, and the hands.

As he was about to put the last touches on the fingertips, Geppetto felt his wig being pulled off. His yellow wig was in the marionette's hand. "Pinocchio, give me my wig!" he cried.

But instead of giving it back, Pinocchio put it on his own head.

Geppetto became very sad and cried out:

"Pinocchio, you wicked boy! You are not yet finished and you start out by being impudent to your poor old father. Very bad, my son, very bad!"

And he wiped away a tear.

The legs and feet still had to be made. As soon as they were done, Geppetto felt a sharp kick on the tip of his nose.

"I deserve it!" he said to himself. "I should have thought of this before I made him. Now it's too late!"

He took hold of the marionette under the arms and put him on the floor to teach him to walk.

Pinocchio's legs were so stiff that he could not move them, but Geppetto held his hand and showed him how to put out one foot after the other.

When his legs were limbered up, Pinocchio started walking by himself, and ran all around the room. He came to the open door, and with one leap he was out onto the street. Away he flew!

Poor Geppetto ran after him but was unable to keep up.

"Catch him! Catch him!" Geppetto kept shouting. But the people in the street, seeing a wooden marionette running like the wind, stood still to stare and laugh.

At last, by sheer luck, a policeman happened along, grabbed Pinocchio by the nose, and returned him to Master Geppetto.

Geppetto seized Pinocchio by the back of the neck to take him home. As he was doing so, he shook Pinocchio two or three times and said to him angrily:

"We're going home now. When we get home, then we'll settle this matter!"

Pinocchio, on hearing this, threw himself on the ground and refused to take another step. Many people gathered around.

"Poor marionette," called out a man. "I am not surprised he doesn't want to go home. Geppetto, no doubt, will beat him unmercifully, he is so mean and cruel!"

"Geppetto looks like a good man," added another, "but with boys he's a real tyrant. If we leave that poor marionette in his hands he may tear him to pieces!"

They said so much that, finally, the policeman ended matters by setting Pinocchio at liberty and dragging Geppetto to prison.

Pinocchio ran home. Upon reaching home, he slipped into the room, locked the door, and threw himself on the floor, happy at his escape.

But his happiness lasted only a short time, for just then he heard someone saying: "Cri-cri-cri!"

"Who is calling me?" asked Pinocchio, greatly frightened.

"I am!"

Pinocchio turned and saw a large cricket crawling slowly up the wall.

"Tell me, cricket, who are you?"

"I am the Talking Cricket and I have been living in this room for more than one hundred years."

"Today, however, this room is mine," said the marionette, "and if you wish to do me a favor, get out now, and don't turn around even once."

"I refuse to leave this spot," answered the cricket, "until I have told you a great truth."

"Tell it, then, and hurry."

"Woe to boys who refuse to obey their parents and run away from home! They will never be happy in this world, and when they are older they will be very sorry for it."

"Sing on cricket, as you please. What I know is that tomorrow, at dawn, I leave this place forever. If I stay here the same thing will happen to me which happens to all other boys and girls. They are sent to school to study. Let me tell you, I hate to study! It's much more fun, I think, to chase after butterflies, climb trees, and steal birds' nests."

"Poor little silly! Don't you know that if you go on like that, you will grow into a perfect donkey and that you'll be the laughingstock of everyone?"

"Keep still, you ugly cricket!" cried Pinocchio.

But the cricket continued:

"If you do not like going to school, why don't you at least learn a trade, so that you can earn an honest living?"

"Shall I tell you something?" asked Pinocchio, who was beginning to lose patience. "Of all the trades in the world, there is only one that really suits me: that of eating, drinking, sleeping, playing, and wandering around from morning till night."

"Those who follow that trade always end up in the hospital or in prison," said the cricket. I feel sorry for you, because you are a marionette and, what is much worse, you have a wooden head."

At these last words, Pinocchio jumped up in a fury, took a hammer from the bench, and threw it with all his strength at the Talking Cricket.

Perhaps he did not think he would strike it, but he hit the cricket straight on its head.

With a last weak "cri-cri-cri" the poor cricket fell from the wall, dead!

If the cricket's death scared Pinocchio at all, it was only for a very few moments. For, as night came on, Pinocchio grew hungry, and realized he had eaten nothing as of yet.

Pinocchio's hunger grew until he was as ravenous as a bear. He searched about the room. Finding nothing, he decided to go out for a walk in the near-by village, in the hope of finding some charitable person who might give him a bit of bread.

But the village was dark and deserted, and he returned home tired, wet, and hungry.

As he no longer had any strength left with which to stand, he sat down on a little stool and put his two feet on the stove to dry them.

There he fell asleep, and while he slept, his wooden feet began to burn. Slowly, they blackened and turned to ashes.

Pinocchio snored away happily as if his feet were not his own. At dawn he opened his eyes just as a loud knocking sounded at the door.

"Who is it?" he called, yawning and rubbing his eyes.

"It is I," answered Geppetto.

The poor marionette, who was still half-asleep, had not yet found out that his two feet were burned off. As soon as he heard his father's voice, he jumped up from his seat to open the door, but, as he did so, he staggered and fell headlong to the floor.

"Open the door for me!" Geppetto shouted from the street.

"Father, dear Father, I can't," answered Pinocchio in despair, crying and rolling on the floor. "Someone has eaten my feet."

Geppetto, thinking that all these tears and cries were only pranks, climbed up the side of the house and went in through the window.

At first he was very angry, but on seeing Pinocchio stretched out on the floor without feet, he felt very sad and sorrowful. Picking him up from the floor, he cried:

"My little Pinocchio, my dear little Pinocchio! How did you burn your feet?"

Pinocchio told Geppetto of his adventures, and that he was still very hungry.

Geppetto gave Pinocchio three pears, which were supposed to be for his breakfast. Pinocchio would not eat the pears unless they were peeled. Geppetto peeled the pears and gave them back to Pinocchio, who devoured them, then began to grumble that he wanted a new pair of feet. He promised not to run away from home again, to study, and to be a good boy.

Master Geppetto made two new feet for Pinocchio. As soon as the marionette felt his new feet, he jumped with joy.

"To show you how grateful I am to you, Father, I'll go to school now. But to go to school I need a suit of clothes."

Geppetto did not have a penny in his pocket, so he made his son a little suit of paper, a pair of shoes from the bark of a tree, and a tiny cap from a bit of dough.

"In order to go to school, I need an A–B–C book," said Pinocchio.

Geppetto then sold his only coat to buy the book for his son.

Pinocchio, unable to restrain his tears, jumped on his father's neck and kissed him over and over.

Pinocchio hurried to school, thinking of the fantastic things he would learn. As he walked, there came the sound of pipes and drums in the distance.

He stopped to listen. The sounds came from a small village along the shore. Pinocchio said to himself:

"Today I'll follow the pipes, and tomorrow I'll go to school. There's always plenty of time to go to school."

He ran toward the sounds, and the pipe and drum grew louder.

Suddenly he found himself in a large square, full of people standing in front of a little wooden building painted in brilliant colors. It was a Marionette Theater. It cost four pennies to get in.

Pinocchio, who was curious to know what was going on inside, sold his schoolbook to a ragpicker nearby for the price of a ticket.

Pinocchio ran into the Marionette Theater. The curtain was up and the performance had started. Harlequin and Pulcinella were reciting on the stage and, as usual, they were threatening each other with sticks and blows.

The theater was full of people, enjoying the spectacle and laughing at the antics of the two marionettes.

The play continued for a few minutes, and then suddenly Harlequin stopped talking. Turning toward the audience, he pointed to the rear of the orchestra, yelling wildly at the same time:

"Look, look! Am I asleep or awake? Do I really see Pinocchio there?"

"Yes, yes! It is Pinocchio!" screamed Pulcinella.

"It is! It is!" shrieked Signora Rosaura, peeking in from the side of the stage.

"It is Pinocchio!" yelled all the marionettes, pouring out of the wings. "It is our brother Pinocchio! Hurrah for Pinocchio!"

"Pinocchio, come up to me!" shouted Harlequin. "Come to the arms of your wooden brothers!"

Pinocchio leaped onto the stage.

The marionettes greeted him with shrieks of joy, warm embraces, knocks, and friendly greetings.

The audience, seeing that the play had stopped, became angry and began to yell: "The play, the play, we want the play!"

The yelling was of no use, for the marionettes just made more noise and, lifting up Pinocchio on their shoulders, carried him around the stage in triumph.

At that very moment, the director came out of his room. He had a fearful appearance: a long black beard, a mouth as wide as an oven, teeth like yellow fangs, and two eyes like glowing red coals. In his huge, hairy hands was a long whip.

Everyone was scared at the unexpected apparition.

"Why have you brought such excitement into my theater?" the huge fellow angrily asked Pinocchio.

"Believe me, your Honor, the fault was not mine."

"Enough! Be quiet! I'll take care of you later."

As soon as the play was over, the director went to the kitchen, where a fine big lamb was cooking. He needed more wood, so he told Harlequin and Pulcinella to bring Pinocchio to him, to use as firewood.

Harlequin and Pulcinella hesitated, but they were afraid of their master and followed his orders. They returned carrying poor Pinocchio, who was wriggling and squirming and crying pitifully:

"Father, save me! I don't want to die! I don't want to die!"

When Fire Eater (this was really his name) saw the poor marionette being brought in to him, struggling with fear and crying, he felt sorry for him and began to sneeze. Fire Eater, instead of crying, sneezed when he felt sad.

Fire Eater then set Pinocchio free. He gave Pinocchio five gold pieces to bring home to his poor old father, Geppetto.

Pinocchio, beside himself with joy, set out toward home.

He had gone barely half a mile when he met a lame fox and a blind cat. The lame fox leaned on the cat, and the blind cat let the fox lead him along.

"Good morning, Pinocchio," said the fox, greeting him courteously.

"How do you know my name?" asked the marionette.

"I know your father well."

"Where have you seen him?"

"I saw him yesterday standing at the door of his house."

"And what was he doing?"

"He was in his shirt sleeves trembling with cold."

"Poor Father! But, after today, God willing, he will suffer no longer."

"Why?"

"Because I have become a rich man."

"You, a rich man?" said the fox, and he began to laugh out loud. The cat was laughing also, but tried to hide it by stroking his long whiskers.

"There is nothing to laugh at," cried Pinocchio angrily. "I am very sorry to make your mouth water, but these, as you know, are five new gold pieces."

And he pulled out the gold pieces which Fire Eater had given him.

At the cheerful tinkle of the gold, the fox unconsciously held out his paw that was supposed to be lame, and the cat opened wide his two eyes till they looked like live coals, but he closed them again so quickly that Pinocchio did not notice.

"And may I ask," inquired the fox, "what you are going to do with all that money?"

"First of all," answered the marionette, "I want to buy a fine new coat for my father, and after that, I'll buy an A-B-C book for myself."

Suddenly, the fox stopped in his tracks and, turning to the marionette, said to him:

"Do you want to double your gold pieces?"

"Yes, but how?" asked Pinocchio.

"Instead of returning home, come with us to the City of Simple Simons. There you can bury your money in a field and overnight your gold pieces will grow into a tree, which is loaded with gold pieces."

Pinocchio agreed to go with the fox and the cat, to grow a tree with many more gold pieces than he already had.

Cat and fox and Pinocchio walked until evening. At last, dead tired, they came to the Inn of the Red Lobster.

"Let us stop here a while," said the fox, "to eat a bite and rest. At midnight we'll start out again, for at dawn tomorrow we must be at the Field of Wonders."

They went into the Inn and sat down to supper.

When supper was done the fox said to the Innkeeper: "Give us two good rooms, one for Mr. Pinocchio and the other for me and my friend. Remember to call us at midnight sharp, for we must continue on our journey."

"Yes, sir," answered the Innkeeper, winking at the fox and the cat.

As soon as Pinocchio was in bed, he slept and dreamed of a tree of gold coins.

In the middle of his dream, Pinocchio was awakened by three loud knocks at the door. The Innkeeper had come to tell him that midnight had struck.

"Are my friends ready?" the marionette asked him.

"Indeed, yes! They went two hours ago. The cat received a telegram which said that his first-born was sick. He could not even wait to say good-bye to you."

"Did they pay for the supper?"

"How could they do that? They did not want to offend by not allowing you the honor of paying. They said to meet them at the Field of Wonders, at sunrise."

Pinocchio paid a gold piece for the three suppers and started on his way.

As he walked, Pinocchio noticed a tiny insect glowing on the trunk of a tree.

"Who are you?" he asked.

"I am the Ghost of the Talking Cricket," answered the little being in a faint voice that sounded as if it came from a far-away world. "I want to give you a few words of good advice. Return home and give the four gold pieces you have left to your poor old father who is weeping because he has not seen you for many a day."

"Tomorrow he will be rich. These four gold pieces will become two thousand."

"Don't listen to those who promise you wealth overnight, my boy. As a rule they are either fools or swindlers! Listen to me and go home."

"But I want to go on!"

"Boys who insist on having their own way sooner or later come to grief."

There was silence for a minute and the light of the Talking Cricket disappeared as if someone had snuffed it out. Once again the road was plunged into darkness.

Pinocchio continued walking until he heard a slight rustle among the leaves.

Two figures, wrapped in black sacks, leaped toward him as if they were ghosts.

"Here they come!" Pinocchio said to himself, and, not knowing where to hide the gold pieces, he stuck all four of them under his tongue.

He tried to run away, but hardly had he taken a step, when he felt his arms grasped and heard two horrible, deep voices say to him: "Your money or your life!"

On account of the gold pieces in his mouth, Pinocchio could not say a word, so he tried with head and hands and body to show, as best he could, that he was only a poor marionette without a penny in his pocket.

"Come, come, less nonsense, and out with your money!" cried the two thieves.

Once more, Pinocchio's head and hands said, "I haven't a penny."

"Out with that money or you're a dead man," said the taller of the two assassins. And after having killed you, we will kill your father also."

"No, no, not my Father!" cried Pinocchio, wild with terror; but as he screamed, the gold pieces tinkled together in his mouth.

"You rascal! You have the money hidden under your tongue. Out with it!"

One of them grabbed the marionette by the nose and the other by the chin, and they pulled him unmercifully from side to side in order to make him open his mouth.

But the marionette's lips might as well have been nailed together. They would not open.

In desperation the smaller of the two assassins pulled out a long knife from his pocket, and tried to pry Pinocchio's mouth open with it.

Quick as a flash, the marionette sank his teeth deep into the assassin's hand, bit it off and spat it out. He was surprised to see it was not a hand, but a cat's paw.

Pinocchio freed himself from the claws of his assailers and, leaping over the bushes along the road, ran swiftly across the fields. His pursuers were after him at once.

After running many miles, Pinocchio was exhausted. He was afraid he would have to surrender to his pursuers. Suddenly he saw a little cottage gleaming white among the trees of the forest.

Pinocchio reached the door of the cottage and knocked. No one answered.

He knocked again, harder than before, for behind him he heard the steps and the labored breathing of his persecutors. The same silence followed.

In despair, Pinocchio began to kick and bang against the door. At the noise, a window opened and a lovely maiden looked out. She had azure hair and a face white as wax. Her eyes were closed and her hands crossed on her breast. With a voice so weak that it hardly could be heard, she whispered:

"Go away. No one here can help you."

After these words, the little girl disappeared and the window closed without a sound.

"Oh, Lovely Maiden with Azure Hair," cried Pinocchio, "open, I beg of you. Take pity on a poor boy who is being chased by two assass—"

He did not finish, for two powerful hands grasped him by the neck and the same two horrible voices growled threateningly: "Now we have you! We will hang you until you drop the coins."

Pinocchio trembled. The two assassins hung the marionette on a tree and waited for Pinocchio to die. Little by little, Pinocchio's eyes closed. As he was about to die, he thought of his poor old father, and said:

"Oh, Father, dear Father! If you were only here!"

Luckily, the lovely maiden with azure hair once again looked out of her window. Filled with pity at the sight of poor Pinocchio, she clapped her hands sharply together three times. A falcon appeared, who flew to Pinocchio and brought him to the fairy (for the lovely maiden with azure hair was none other than a very kind fairy who had lived, for more than a thousand years, in the vicinity of the forest).

The fairy put Pinocchio to bed and called for Crow, Owl, and Talking Cricket, who were the best doctors in the neighborhood. The crow pronounced the marionette dead, but the owl said that he was alive.

The cricket said: "I say that a wise doctor, when he does not know what he is talking about, should know enough to keep his mouth shut. However, I know this marionette. He is a vagabond and a runaway."

Pinocchio, who until then had been very quiet, shuddered so hard that the bed shook.

"The marionette is a disobedient son who is breaking his father's heart!"

Pinocchio hid his face under the sheets and sobbed.

"When the dead weep, they are beginning to recover," said the crow solemnly.

"I disagree," said the owl, "I think that when the dead weep, it means they do not want to die."

As soon as the three doctors had left the room, the fairy touched Pinocchio on the forehead, and noticed that he was burning with fever.

She handed Pinocchio medicine, saying lovingly to him:

"Drink this, and in a few days you'll be up and well."

Pinocchio did not want to drink the medicine because it was bitter, but the fairy said that if he did not drink it he would die. So Pinocchio drank the liquid. In a twinkling, he felt fine. With one leap he was out of bed and into his clothes.

The fairy, seeing him run and jump around the room gay as a bird on wing, said to him:

"My medicine was good for you, after all, wasn't it?"

"Good indeed! It has given me new life."

"Come here now and tell me how it came about that you found yourself in the hands of the assassins."

Pinocchio told the fairy his story, and that he had lost his gold pieces. That was a lie, for he had them in his pocket.

As he spoke, his nose grew longer. The more he lied, the more it grew.

The fairy sat looking at him and laughing.

"Why do you laugh?" the marionette asked her, worried now at the sight of his growing nose.

"I am laughing at your lies."

"How do you know I am lying?"

"Lies, my boy, are known in a moment. There are two kinds of lies, lies with short legs and lies with long noses. Yours, just now, happen to have long noses."

Pinocchio, not knowing where to hide his shame, tried to escape from the room, but his nose had become so long that he could not get it out of the door.

The fairy felt sorry for him and called for a thousand woodpeckers to peck away his nose, so that it was the same size as before.

"How good you are, my fairy," said Pinocchio, "and how much I love you!"

"I love you, too," answered the fairy, "and if you wish to stay with me, you may be my little brother and I'll be your good little sister."

"I should like to stay—but what about my poor father?"

"Your father has been sent for and before night he will be here."

"Really?" cried Pinocchio joyfully. "Then, my good fairy, if you are willing, I should like to go to meet him. I cannot wait to kiss that dear old man, who has suffered so much for my sake."

"Surely; go ahead, but be careful not to lose your way. Take the wood path and you'll surely meet him."

Pinocchio set out, and soon ran into the fox and cat. He foolishly agreed to continue on with them to the Field of Wonders.

They walked and walked for half a day and at last came to the town called the City of Simple Simons. It was filled with mangy animals.

Through this crowd of poor animals, a beautiful coach passed now and again. Within it sat either a fox, a hawk, or a vulture.

Pinocchio, fox, and cat passed through the city and, just outside the walls, they stepped into a field, which looked like any other field. Pinocchio buried his gold pieces and went away for twenty minutes as the fox told him to, so that his tree could grow.

Upon returning, Pinocchio saw that there was no tree, and that his coins had been dug up. The fox and cat had robbed him.

In desperation, he ran to the city and went straight to the courthouse to report the robbery to the magistrate. The judge was a large gorilla, venerable with age. A flowing white beard covered his chest and he wore gold-rimmed spectacles from which the glasses had dropped out.

Pinocchio told the judge his pitiful tale. When the marionette had no more to say, the judge rang a bell.

At the sound, two large dogs appeared, dressed in policemens' uniforms.

Then the magistrate, pointing to Pinocchio, said in a very solemn voice:

"This poor simpleton has been robbed of four gold pieces. Take him, therefore, and throw him into prison."

The marionette, on hearing this sentence passed upon him, was thoroughly stunned. He tried to protest, but the two officers clapped their paws on his mouth and hustled him away to jail.

There he had to remain for four months. When he was released, Pinocchio ran away from the city, to find the house of the lovely fairy. He was determined to see his father and his fairy, and to become a good boy.

Pinocchio finally came to the spot where the fairy's house had once stood. It was no longer there. In its place lay a small marble slab, which bore this sad inscription:

Here lies the lovely fairy with azure hair
who died of grief when abandoned by her little brother Pinocchio

The poor marionette was heartbroken at reading these words, and burst into bitter tears. He cried all night, until a pigeon flew by in the morning and carried him to the seashore, where his father, Geppetto, had been looking for him. Geppetto had been searching for his son for a long time.

Upon arriving at the seashore, Pinocchio spotted a little boat tossing amongst the wild waves of the rough sea. It was his father, Geppetto! Pinocchio stood on a high rock and waved and cried out to his father.

It looked as if Geppetto, though far away from the shore, recognized his son, for he took off his cap and waved also. Suddenly a huge wave came and the boat disappeared.

Pinocchio jumped into the sea and cried out:

"I'll save him! I'll save my father!"

The marionette, being made of wood, floated easily along and swam like a fish in the rough water. In a twinkling, he was far away from land.

Pinocchio, spurred on by the hope of finding his father and of being in time to save him, swam all night long. In the morning he saw an island and, tired and soaked, stopped to rest.

The marionette took off his clothes and laid them on the sand to dry. He looked over the waters for his father. He searched and searched, but saw nothing except sea and sky.

A dolphin, swimming by, told Pinocchio that his father had probably been swallowed up by the huge shark that had recently been invading the waters. He also told Pinocchio how to get to the nearest village, where he could get some food.

This said, Pinocchio headed toward the village.

In the village, everyone was busy working.

A little woman went by carrying two water jugs.

"Good woman, will you allow me to have a drink from one of your jugs?" asked Pinocchio, who was burning up with thirst.

"With pleasure, my boy!" she answered, setting the two jugs on the ground before him.

When Pinocchio had had his fill, he grumbled, as he wiped his mouth:

"My thirst is gone. If I could only as easily get rid of my hunger!"

On hearing these words, the good little woman immediately said:

"If you help me to carry these jugs home, I'll give you a slice of bread, some cauliflower with white sauce, cake and jam."

Pinocchio said: "Very well. I'll take the jug home for you."

The jug was very heavy, and the marionette, not being strong enough to carry it with his hands, had to put it on his head.

When they arrived home, the little woman made Pinocchio sit down at a small table and placed before him the bread, the cauliflower, and the cake. Pinocchio devoured it. His stomach seemed a bottomless pit.

His hunger finally appeased, he raised his head to thank his kind benefactress. But he had not looked at her long when he gave a cry of surprise. The woman was his little fairy!

"You rascal of a marionette! How did you know it was I?" she asked, laughing.

"My love for you told me who you were."

"Do you remember? You left me when I was a little girl and now you find me a grown woman. I am so old, I could almost be your mother!"

"I am very glad of that, for then I can call you mother instead of sister. For a long time I have wanted a mother, just like other boys. But how did you grow so quickly?"

"That's a secret!"

"Tell it to me. I also want to grow a little."

"But you can't grow," answered the fairy. "Marionettes never grow. They are born marionettes, they live as marionettes, and they die as marionettes."

"Oh, I'm tired of always being a marionette!" cried Pinocchio disgustedly. "It's about time for me to grow into a man as everyone else does."

"And you will if you deserve it—"

"Really? What can I do to deserve it?"

"If you are good, if you go to school and study and do not tell lies, you can become a real boy," answered the fairy.

"I promise. I want to become a good boy and be a comfort to my father. Where is my poor father now?"

"I do not know."

"Will I ever be lucky enough to find him and embrace him once more?"

"I think so. Indeed, I am sure of it."

At this answer, Pinocchio's happiness was very great. He grasped the fairy's hands and kissed them hard.

The fairy had forgiven Pinocchio for running away. She said: "From now on, I'll be your own little mother.

"Oh! How lovely!" cried Pinocchio, jumping with joy.

"Beginning tomorrow," said the fairy, "you'll go to school every day."

Pinocchio finally agreed, for he wanted to be a real boy.

In the morning, bright and early, Pinocchio went to school.

The boys in the classroom laughed and played tricks on him. But they did not play tricks for long, for Pinocchio gave one of the boys a sound kick with his wooden foot, and a jab with his elbow, which made the boys favor Pinocchio after that.

As the days passed into weeks, even the teacher praised him, for he saw him attentive, hard working, and wide awake, always the first to come in the morning, and the last to leave when school was over.

Pinocchio's only fault was that he had too many friends who were well-known rascals, who cared not a bit for study or for success.

The teacher warned him each day, and even the good fairy repeated to him many times:

"Take care, Pinocchio! Those bad companions will sooner or later make you lose your love for study. Some day they will lead you astray."

"There's no such danger," answered the marionette, shrugging his shoulders and pointing to his forehead as if to say, "I'm too wise."

So it happened that one day, as he was walking to school, he met some boys who ran up to him and said:

"Have you heard the news?"

"No!"

"A shark as big as a mountain has been seen near the shore."

"Really? I wonder if it could be the same one I heard of when my father was drowned?"

"We are going to see it. Are you coming?"

"No, not I. I must go to school."

"What do you care about school? You can go there tomorrow."

"Do you know what I'll do?" said Pinocchio. "For certain reasons of mine, I, too, want to see that shark; but I'll go after school. I can see him then as well as now."

"Poor simpleton!" cried one of the boys. "Do you think that a fish of that size will stand there waiting for you? He turns and off he goes, and no one will ever be the wiser."

"How long does it take from here to the shore?" asked Pinocchio.

"One hour there and back."

"Very well, then. Let's see who gets there first!" cried Pinocchio.

At the signal, the little troop, with books under their arms, dashed across the fields. Pinocchio led the way, running as if on wings, the others following as fast as they could.

Going like the wind, Pinocchio took but a very short time to reach the shore. He glanced all about him, but there was no sign of a shark. The sea was as smooth as glass.

The boys had played a trick on him.

"What now?" he said angrily to them. "What's the joke?"

"Oh, the joke's on you!" cried his tormentors, laughing more heartily than ever, and dancing gayly around the marionette.

"And that is—?"

"That we have made you stay out of school to come with us. Aren't you ashamed of being such a goody-goody, and of studying so hard? You never have a bit of enjoyment."

The boys went on tormenting Pinocchio, and they eventually started to fight with him. They threw books at him. One book hit another boy, named Eugene, in the head. Eugene, pale as a ghost, cried out faintly:

"Oh, Mother, help! I'm dying!" and fell senseless to the ground.

All the boys except Pinocchio were scared and ran away. Pinocchio called to him, saying: "Eugene! My poor Eugene! Open your eyes and look at me! Why don't you answer?"

Pinocchio went on crying and moaning. Again and again he called to his little friend, when suddenly he heard heavy steps approaching.

He looked up and saw two tall policemen near him. Thinking Pinocchio had hurt the boy with his schoolbook, they told Pinocchio:

"Get up as quickly as you can and come along with us."

"But I am innocent."

"Come with us!"

Before starting out, the officers called out to several fishermen passing by in a boat and said to them:

"Take care of this little fellow who has been hurt. Take him home and bind his wounds. Tomorrow we'll come for him."

They then took hold of Pinocchio and, putting him between them, said to him in a rough voice:

"March! And go quickly, or it will be the worse for you!"

They did not have to repeat their words. The marionette walked swiftly along the road to the village, but he suffered at the thought of passing under the windows of his good little fairy's house. What would she say on seeing him between two policemen?

They had just reached the village, when a sudden gust of wind blew off Pinocchio's cap and made it go sailing far down the street.

"Would you allow me," the marionette asked the policemen, "to run after my cap?"

"Very well, go; but hurry."

The marionette went, picked up his cap—but instead of putting it on his head, he stuck it between his teeth and raced toward the sea.

The policemen, judging that it would be very difficult to catch him, sent a large dog after him, one that had won first prize in all the dog races. Pinocchio ran fast and the dog ran faster.

The dog, named Alidoro, had almost caught Pinocchio, when the marionette made a great leap into the sea.

Alidoro tried to stop, but as he was running very fast, he couldn't, and he, too, landed far out in the sea. The dog could not swim. He beat the water with his paws to hold himself up, but the harder he tried, the deeper he sank. As he stuck his head out once more, the poor fellow's eyes were bulging and he barked out wildly, "I drown! Help, Pinocchio! Save me from death!"

At those cries of suffering, the marionette, who after all had a very kind heart, was moved to compassion. He turned toward the poor animal and said to him:

"But if I help you, will you promise not to bother me again by running after me?"

"I promise! Only hurry, for if you wait another second, I'll be dead and gone!"

Pinocchio caught hold of Alidoro's tail and dragged him to shore.

The poor dog was so weak he could not stand. He had swallowed so much salt water that he was swollen like a balloon. However, Pinocchio, not wishing to trust him too much, threw himself once again into the sea. As he swam away, he called out:

"Good-bye, Alidoro, good luck and remember me to your family!"

"Good-bye, little Pinocchio," answered the dog. "A thousand thanks for having saved me from death. You did me a good turn, and, in this world, what is given is always returned. If the chance comes, I shall be there."

Pinocchio went on swimming close to shore. At last he thought he had reached a safe place. Glancing up and down the beach, he saw the opening of a cave out of which rose a spiral of smoke.

Suddenly he felt something under him lifting him up higher and higher. Pinocchio was in a huge net, amid a crowd of fish of all kinds and sizes, who were fighting and struggling desperately to free themselves.

At the same time, he saw a fisherman come out of the cave, a fisherman so ugly that Pinocchio thought he was a sea monster. In place of hair, his head was covered by a thick bush of green grass. His skin was green, his eyes were green, and his long beard was green.

When the fisherman pulled the net out of the sea, he cried out joyfully:

"Blessed Providence! Once more I'll have a fine meal of fish!"

The fisherman took the net and the fish into the dark cave. In the middle of it, a pan full of oil sizzled over a smoky fire. The fisherman covered the fish in flour, and began to place them in the sizzling pan.

The last to come out of the net was Pinocchio.

As soon as the fisherman pulled him out, his green eyes opened wide with surprise, and he cried out in fear:

"What kind of fish is this? I don't remember ever eating anything like it."

"I am a marionette," said Pinocchio, "I am not a fish."

The fisherman decided to eat Pinocchio anyway. He rolled him in flour and got ready to put Pinocchio in the frying pan. Pinocchio trembled with fright.

Just then a large dog, attracted by the odor of the boiling oil, came running into the cave.

"Get out!" cried the fisherman threateningly, still holding onto the marionette, who was covered with flour.

But the poor dog was very hungry, and whining and wagging his tail, he tried to say:

"Give me a bite of the fish and I'll go in peace."

"Get out, I say!" repeated the fisherman.

And he drew back his foot to give the dog a kick.

Then the dog, who, being really hungry, would take no refusal, turned in a rage toward the fisherman and bared his terrible fangs. And at that moment, a pitiful little voice was heard saying: "Save me, Alidoro; if you don't, I fry!"

The dog immediately recognized Pinocchio's voice. Great was his surprise to find that the voice came from the little flour-covered bundle that the fisherman held in his hand.

With one great leap, Alidero grasped that bundle in his mouth and, holding it tightly between his teeth, ran through the door and disappeared.

The fisherman, angry at seeing his meal snatched from under his nose, ran after the dog, but a bad fit of coughing made him stop and turn back.

Meanwhile, Alidoro, as soon as he had found the road which led to the village, stopped and dropped Pinocchio softly to the ground.

"How much I do thank you!" said the marionette.

"It is not necessary," answered the dog. "You saved me once, and what is given is always returned. We are in this world to help one another."

They bid each other farewell as good friends.

Pinocchio, left alone, walked toward a little hut near by, where an old man sat at the door sunning himself, and asked:

"Tell me, good man, have you heard anything of a poor boy with a wounded head, whose name was Eugene?"

"The boy was brought to this hut. He is alive and has already returned home."

Pinocchio was overjoyed at hearing this news. He set out at once to return to the fairy's house. Upon reaching the house, Pinocchio was so tired that he fell asleep on the doorstep.

When he awoke, Pinocchio found himself stretched out on a sofa and the fairy was seated near him.

"This time also I forgive you," said the fairy to him. "But be careful not to get into mischief again."

Pinocchio promised to study and to behave himself. And he kept his word for the remainder of the year. At the end of it, he passed first in all his examinations, and his report was so good that the fairy said to him happily:

"Tomorrow your wish will come true."

"And what is it?"

"Tomorrow you will cease to be a marionette and will become a real boy."

Pinocchio was beside himself with joy. All his friends and schoolmates must be invited to celebrate the great event. He went to give out invitations.

When Pinocchio went to look for Lamp-Wick, the laziest boy in school, he could not find him.

Finally he discovered Lamp-Wick hiding near a farmer's wagon.

"What are you doing there?" asked Pinocchio, running up to him.

"I am waiting for midnight to strike to go far-away to the Land of Toys. A place where there is no school and you play all day long. Why don't you come, too?"

"I? Oh, no! But I will wait here to see you go."

Finally the wagon arrived, packed with boys.

It was drawn by twenty-four donkeys, all wearing shoes made of leather, just like the ones boys wear.

The driver of the wagon was a jolly fat man, with a small and wheedling voice.

No sooner had the wagon stopped than the little fat man turned to Lamp-Wick. With bows and smiles, he asked:

"Tell me, my fine boy, do you also want to come to my wonderful country?"

"Indeed I do."

"Hope on the top of the coach then."

To Pinocchio he said:

"What about you, my love?"

Pinocchio hesitated, but with much prodding from Lamp-Wick, finally agreed to go. There were no seats left, so Pinocchio had to ride one of the donkeys. The donkey did not like it at first, but the man finally made the donkey allow Pinocchio to ride it.

While the donkeys galloped along the stony road, the marionette thought he heard a very quiet voice whispering to him:

"Poor silly! You have done as you wished. But you are going to be a sorry boy before very long. A day will come when you will weep bitterly, even as I am weeping now—but it will be too late!"

At these whispered words, Pinocchio grew more and more frightened. He jumped to the ground, ran up to the donkey on whose back he had been riding, and taking his nose in his hands, looked at him. He saw that the donkey was weeping—just like a boy!

"Hey, Mr. Driver!" cried the marionette. "Do you know what strange thing is happening here! This donkey weeps."

"Let him weep. Ignore it and ride along."

Pinocchio obeyed, and toward dawn the wagon finally reached the Land of Toys.

The population of this land was composed wholly of boys. The oldest were about fourteen years of age, the youngest, eight. In the street was a racket from boys shouting and blowing trumpets. Everywhere boys were playing games, such as marbles, tag, ball, and circus. Generals in full uniform led regiments of cardboard soldiers. Everywhere there was great pandemonium and laughter.

The squares were filled with small wooden theaters, overflowing with boys from morning till night, and on the walls of the houses were the words:

**HURRAH FOR THE LAND OF TOYS!
DOWN WITH ARITHMETIC! NO MORE SCHOOL!**

As soon as they had set foot in that land, Pinocchio, Lamp-Wick, and all the other boys who had traveled with them started out on a tour of investigation. They wandered everywhere, and became everybody's friend.

What with entertainments and parties, the hours, the days, the weeks passed like lightning.

Five months passed and the boys continued playing and enjoying themselves from morning till night, without ever going to school.

One morning, after five months had past, Pinocchio awoke to find that his ears had grown at least ten full inches, into donkey's ears!

He began to cry and scream, but the more he shrieked, the longer and the more hairy his ears grew. Pinocchio put a bag over his head, and went out to find his friend Lamp-Wick. He thought that Lamp-Wick was to blame for bringing him to the Land of Toys in the first place.

With his head covered he went out. He looked everywhere for Lamp-Wick, but he was not to be found. He asked everyone whom he met about him, but no one had seen him. In desperation, Pinocchio returned home and knocked at the door.

"Who is it?" asked Lamp-Wick from within.

"It is I!" answered the marionette.

"Wait a minute."

After a full half hour the door opened. There in the room stood Lamp-Wick, with a bag over his head.

At the sight of that bag, Pinocchio realized that Lamp-Wick was, indeed, turning into a donkey as well. They threw off their bags and, instead of feeling sorry for each other, the friends made fun of one another.

They laughed and laughed, and laughed again—laughed till they ached—laughed till they cried.

But all of a sudden Lamp-Wick stopped laughing. He tottered and almost fell. Pale as a ghost, he turned to Pinocchio and said:

"Help, Pinocchio! I can no longer stand up."

"I can't either," cried Pinocchio; and his laughter turned to tears as he stumbled about helplessly.

They had hardly finished speaking, when both of them fell on all fours and began running and jumping around the room. As they ran, their arms turned into legs, their faces lengthened into snouts, their backs became covered with long gray hairs, and they grew tails.

Instead of moans and cries, they burst forth into loud donkey brays, which sounded very much like, "Haw! Haw! Haw!"

At that moment, a loud knocking was heard at the door and a voice called to them:

"Open! I am the driver of the wagon which brought you here. Open, I say, or beware!"

Very sad and downcast were the two poor little fellows as they stood and looked at each other. Outside the room, the driver grew more and more impatient, and finally gave the door such a violent kick that it flew open. With his usual sweet smile on his lips, he looked at Pinocchio and Lamp-Wick and said to them:

"Fine work, boys! You have brayed well, so well that I recognized your voices immediately, and here I am."

The man brought them to market to sell. Pinocchio was sold to the owner of a circus, who wanted to teach him to do tricks for his audiences.

Pinocchio knew that if he had gone to school and studied hard, he never would have become a circus donkey.

After putting him in a stable, his new master filled his manger with straw, which Pinocchio did not like at first but finally ate because he was very hungry.

His new owner was very mean, and often whipped Pinocchio. He taught Pinocchio to jump and bow, to dance a waltz and a polka, and to stand on his head.

It took poor Pinocchio three long months and cost him many lashings before he was pronounced perfect.

The day came at last when Pinocchio's master was able to announce an extraordinary performance. The announcements, posted all around the town, and written in large letters, read thus:

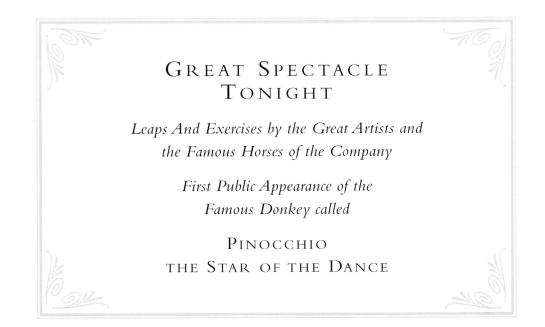

GREAT SPECTACLE
TONIGHT

*Leaps And Exercises by the Great Artists and
the Famous Horses of the Company*

*First Public Appearance of the
Famous Donkey called*

PINOCCHIO
THE STAR OF THE DANCE

That night the theater was filled with boys and girls of all ages and sizes, impatiently waiting to see the famous donkey dance.

The manager of the circus appeared, in a black coat, white knee breeches, and patent leather boots, to announce Pinocchio's dance. Pinocchio then appeared in the circus ring, handsomely adorned, to do tricks for the audience. Near the end of his act, he fell down and became lame, barely able to limp back to his stable.

The next morning the veterinarian declared that Pinocchio would be lame for the rest of his life.

"What do I want with a lame donkey?" said the manager to the stableboy. "Take him to the market and sell him."

A buyer was soon found who wanted to use Pinocchio's skin to make a drumhead.

As soon as the buyer had paid for the donkey, he took Pinocchio to a high cliff overlooking the sea, put a stone around his neck, tied a rope to one of his hind feet, and threw him into the water.

Pinocchio sank immediately. His new master sat on the cliff waiting for him to drown, so as to skin him and make himself a drumhead.

After fifty minutes of waiting, the man thought his donkey was drowned, and pulled the rope, which he had tied to Pinocchio's leg. The man pulled and pulled, until at last he saw something appear on the surface of the water. But instead of a dead donkey, a very much alive marionette, wriggling and squirming like an eel.

The man could not believe what he saw. What had happened to his donkey?

The fairy had been protecting Pinocchio from drowning, and sent a thousand fish to bite away the part of him that was a donkey. Upon rising to the surface, Pinocchio bid the man farewell and swam off into the sea.

Far off in the sea, Pinocchio suddenly saw a horrible sea monster stick its head out of the water. It had an enormous head with a huge mouth, wide open, showing three rows of gleaming teeth.

Pinocchio tried to swim away, but the sea monster, who was in fact the shark, swallowed him.

When he recovered his senses the marionette could not remember where he was. Around him all was darkness. He listened for a few moments and heard nothing. Once in a while a cold wind blew on his face. At first he could not understand where that wind was coming from, but after a while he understood that it came from the lungs of the monster. The shark was suffering from asthma, so that whenever he breathed a storm seemed to blow.

Pinocchio thought he saw a faint light in the distance. He walked toward the light. The closer he got, the brighter and clearer grew the tiny light. On and on he walked till finally he found a little table set for dinner and lighted by a candle stuck in a glass bottle; near the table sat a little old man, white as the snow, eating live fish.

At this sight, the poor marionette was filled with such great and sudden happiness that he almost dropped in a faint. He wanted to laugh, he wanted to cry, he wanted to say a thousand and one things, but all he could do was to stand still, stuttering and stammering brokenly. At last, with a great effort, he was able to let out a scream of joy and, opening wide his arms he threw them around the old man's neck.

"Oh, Father, dear Father! Have I found you at last? Now I shall never, never leave you again!"

"Are my eyes really telling me the truth?" answered the old man, rubbing his eyes. "Are you really my own dear Pinocchio?"

"Yes, yes, yes! It is I! Look at me! And you have forgiven me, haven't you? Oh, my dear Father, how good you are! And to think that I—oh, but if you only knew how many misfortunes have fallen on my head and how many troubles I have had!"

Pinocchio told his father of his troubles, and Geppetto told Pinocchio of how his boat had been swallowed by the shark.

"There is no time to lose," Pinocchio said, "We must try to escape."

"Escape! How?"

"We can run out of the shark's mouth and dive into the sea. Follow me."

Pinocchio took the candle in his hand, to light the way, and started off on the long walk through the stomach and the whole body of the shark. When they reached the throat of the monster, they stopped for a while to wait for the right moment in which to make their escape.

The shark, being very old and suffering from asthma and heart trouble, was obliged to sleep with his mouth open. Because of this, Pinocchio was able to catch a glimpse of the sky filled with stars, as he looked up through the shark's open jaws.

"The time has come for us to escape," he whispered, turning to his father. "The shark is fast asleep. The sea is calm and the night is as bright as day. Follow me closely, dear Father, and we shall soon be saved."

No sooner said than done. They climbed up the throat of the monster till they came to that immense open mouth. There they had to walk on tiptoes, for if they tickled the shark's long tongue he might awaken. They jumped over three rows of teeth. Before they took the last great leap, the marionette said to his father:

"Climb on my back and hold on tightly to my neck. I'll take care of everything else."

As soon as Geppetto was comfortably seated on his shoulders, Pinocchio dived into the water and started to swim. The shark continued to sleep so soundly that not even a cannon shot would have awakened him.

Pinocchio swam as hard as he could, trying to find shore. After quite a while he began to feel discouraged, and his strength was leaving him. He felt he could not go on much longer, and the shore was still far away.

He swam a few more strokes. Then he turned to Geppetto and cried out weakly:

"Help me, Father! Help, for I am dying!"

Father and son were about to drown when a tunny came up out of the sea, to give them a ride to shore. The tunny had been in the stomach of the shark as well, and followed Pinocchio's example to escape.

Geppetto and Pinocchio climbed on the tunny's back and soon they were on the shore.

In the meantime day had dawned.

Pinocchio offered his arm to Geppetto, who was so weak he could hardly stand, and said to him:

"Lean on my arm, dear father, and let us go find a house or hut, where they will be kind enough to give us a bite of bread and a bit of straw to sleep on. We will walk very slowly, and if we feel tired we can rest by the wayside."

They had not taken a hundred steps when they came upon fox and cat. After pretending to be lame for so many years, the fox had really become lame. The cat, after pretending to be blind for so many years, had really lost the sight of both eyes.

"Oh, Pinocchio," the fox cried in a tearful voice. "Give us some alms, we beg of you! We are old, tired, and sick."

"Sick!" repeated the cat.

"Addio, false friends!" answered the marionette. "You cheated me once, but you will never catch me again. If you are poor; you deserve it! Remember the old proverb which says: `Stolen money never bears fruit.'"

Waving good-bye to them, Pinocchio and Geppetto calmly went on their way. After a few more steps, they saw a tiny cottage built of straw.

They went and knocked at the door.

"Who is it?" said a little voice from within.

"A poor father and a poorer son, without food and with no roof to cover them," answered the marionette.

"Turn the key and the door will open," said the same little voice.

Pinocchio turned the key and the door opened. As soon as they went in, they looked here and there and everywhere but saw no one.

"Oh—ho, where is the owner of the hut?" cried Pinocchio, very much surprised.

"Here I am, up here!"

Father and son looked up to the ceiling, and there on a beam sat the Talking Cricket. The Talking Cricket had forgiven Pinocchio for throwing a hammer at him, and offered a bed of straw to the father and son.

Pinocchio laid his father on it and said to the Talking Cricket:

"Tell me, little cricket, where shall I find a glass of milk for my poor father?"

"Three fields away from here lives Farmer John. He has some cows. Go there and he will give you what you want."

Pinocchio ran all the way to Farmer John's house. The farmer told Pinocchio that if he drew water for him, he would give the marionette a glass of milk.

"Until today," said the farmer, "my donkey has drawn the water for me, but now that poor animal is dying."

"Will you take me to see him?" said Pinocchio.

"Gladly."

Pinocchio spied the little donkey in the stable, and went to him. He asked the donkey: "Who are you?"

At this question, the donkey opened weary, dying eyes and answered: "I am Lamp-Wick."

Then he closed his eyes and died.

"Oh, my poor Lamp-Wick," said Pinocchio in a faint voice, as he wiped his eyes with some straw he had picked up from the ground.

From that day on, for more than five months, Pinocchio got up every morning to work to get a glass of warm milk for his poor old father, who grew stronger and better day by day. But he was not satisfied with this. He learned to make baskets of reeds and sold them. With the money he received, he and his father were able to keep from starving.

One morning Pinocchio saw the fairy's maid. The maid said that the fairy was very ill. Pinocchio gave the maid fifty pennies to give to his poor fairy. He worked harder than ever to help his poor father and his fairy.

In the evening the marionette studied by lamplight. Little by little his diligence was rewarded. He succeeded, not only in his studies, but also in his work, and a day came when he put enough money together to keep his old father comfortable and happy.

One night, as he slept, Pinocchio dreamt of his fairy, who kissed him and said: "Bravo, Pinocchio! Always try to do good, and you will be happy."

At that very moment, Pinocchio awoke. Upon looking himself over, he saw that he was no longer a marionette, but a real live boy! He looked all about him and instead of the usual walls of straw, he found himself in a beautifully furnished little room. Pinocchio ran into the other room, where Geppetto was working at his new bench.

Pinocchio joyfully said: "How ridiculous I was when I was a puppet! And how glad I am now that I have become a real boy!"